This Book belongs to :—

To The
"Dutch Twins"
and their friends —

THE JAPANESE TWINS

By Lucy Fitch Perkins

ILLUSTRATED BY THE AUTHOR

WALKER AND COMPANY
New York

Published in the United States of America
in 1968 by Walker and Company, a division of the
Walker Publishing Company, Inc.

Library of Congress Catalog Card Number: 68-28149

Printed in the United States of America.

CONTENTS

THE JAPANESE TWINS

THE JAPANESE TWINS
AND BŌT'CHAN

Away, away, ever so far away, near the western shores of the Ocean of Peace, lie the Happy Islands, the Paradise of Children.

Some people call this ocean the "Pacific" and they call the Happy Islands "Japan," but the meaning is just the same. Those are only their grown-up names, that you find them by on the map, in the geography.

They are truly Happy Islands, for the sun shines there so brightly that all the people go about with pleasant, smiling faces, and the children play out of doors the whole year through without ever quarreling. And they are never, never spanked! Of course, the reason for that is that they are so good they never, never need it! Or maybe their fathers and mothers do not believe in spanking.

I have even been told — though I don't know whether to think it's true or not — that Japanese

3

parents believe more in sugar-plums than in punish-ments to make children good!

Anyway, the children there are very good indeed.

In a little town near a large city on one of the Happy Islands, there is a garden. In the garden stands a house, and in that House there live Taro, who is a boy, and Take,[1] who is a girl.

They are twins. They are Japanese Twins and they are just five years old, both of them.

Of course, Taro and Take do not live alone in the house in the garden. Their Father and Mother live there too, and their Grandmother, who is very old, and the Baby, who is very young.

Taro and Take cannot remember when Grand-mother and Father and Mother happened, because they were all there when the Twins came; and the Twins could not possibly imagine the world without Father and Mother and Grandmother.

But with the Baby it was different. One day there was n't any Baby at all, and the next day after that, there he was, looking very new but quite at home already in the little house in the garden, where Taro and Take lived.

"Taro" means eldest son, and the Baby might have been called "Jiro," because "Jiro" means

---

[1] Pronounce Tah'-kay.

"second," and he was the second boy in the family; but from the day he came they called him just "Bōt'Chan." That is what they call boy babies in Japan.

"Take" means "bamboo," and the Twins' Father and Mother named their little daughter "Take" because they hoped she would grow up to be tall and slender and strong and graceful like the bamboo tree.

Now, can you think of anything nicer in this world than being Twins, and living with a Mother and Father and Grandmother and a Baby Brother, in a dear little house, in a dear little garden, in a dear little, queer little town in the middle of the Happy Islands that lie in the Ocean of Peace?

Taro and Take thought it was the nicest thing that could possibly have happened; though, as they had n't ever lived anywhere else, or been anybody but themselves for a single minute, I don't see how they could be quite so sure about it.

This book is all about Taro and Take and the Baby, and what a nice time they had living. And if you want to know some of the things that happened on the very first day that the Twins and Bōt'Chan ever saw each other you can turn over to the next page and read about the day the Baby came. That tells all about it, just exactly as it was.

5

I

THE DAY THE BABY CAME

1

THE DAY THE BABY CAME

TARO and Take were standing right beside their Father early one morning when the nurse came into the room with a bundle in her arms.

It was a queer-looking, knobby kind of a bundle, and there was something in it that squirmed!

The nurse looked so happy and smiling that the twins knew at once there must be something very nice in the bundle, but what it was they could not guess.

Taro thought, "Maybe it's a puppy." He had wanted a puppy for a long time.

And Take thought, "Perhaps it's a kitten! But it looks pretty large for a kitten, and it does n't mew. Kittens always mew."

And they both thought, "Anyway, it's alive."

9

The nurse carried the bundle across the room. She knelt down on the floor before the Twins' Father and laid it at his feet.

The Twins' Father looked very much surprised, and as for Taro and Take, they felt just exactly the way you feel when you look at your stocking on Christmas morning.

They dropped down on their knees beside the bundle, one on each side of their Father. They wanted dreadfully to open it. They wanted so dreadfully to open it that they had to hold their hands hard to keep from touching it, but they never even laid a finger on it, because the nurse had given it to their Father!

Taro just said aloud: "Is it a puppy?"

At the very same moment Take said: "Is it a kitten?"

And then their Father said: "I have n't opened the bundle yet, so how can I tell? We must ask the nurse. What is it, Natsu?"

And Natsu, the nurse, put her two hands together on the matting in front of her, bobbed her head down nearly to the floor, and said: "It is a little son, Master. Will you accept him?"

Then the Father sat right down on the floor, too, between Taro and Take. He took the little squirming bundle in his arms, and turned back the covers — and there was a beautiful baby boy, with long, narrow eyes

and a lock of hair that stood straight up
on the top of his head!

"Oh! oh! Is he truly ours—a real live
baby, for us to keep?" cried Take.

"Would you like to keep him?" her
Father asked.

Take clapped her hands for joy. "Oh,
yes, yes!" she said. "For then I can have
a little brother of my own to carry on my

back, just the way O Kiku San carries hers!
I 've never had a thing but borrowed babies
before! And O Kiku San is not polite about
lending hers at all! Please, please let me
hold him!"

She held up her arms, and the Father laid
the little baby in them very, very gently.

Taro was so surprised to see a baby in
the bundle that he had not said a word.
He just sat still and looked astonished.

"Well, Taro, how is it with you?" said

his Father. "Would you like to keep the Baby, too?"

"I'd even rather have him than a puppy!" said Taro very solemnly. And that was a great deal for Taro to say, for he had wanted a puppy for ever so many weeks.

"So would I rather have him than a puppy," the Father said; "ever so much rather."

Just then the Baby puckered up his nose, and opened his little bit of a mouth—and a great big squeal came out of it! You would never have believed that such a big squeal could possibly come out of such a little mouth. And he squirmed more than ever.

Then Natsu, the nurse, said, "There, there, little one! Come to your old Natsu, and she will carry you to Mother again."

"Let me carry him," Take begged.

"No, let me," said Taro.

But Natsu said, "No, no, I will carry him myself. But you may come with me, if you want to, and see your Mother."

So Taro and Take and their Father all
tiptoed quietly into the Mother's room, and
sat down on the floor beside her bed.

They sat on the floor because everybody
sits on the floor in Japan. The bed was on
the floor, too.

It was made of many thick quilts, and the
pillow a little block of wood! We should

think it very uncomfortable, but the Twins' Mother did not think so. She lay with the wooden pillow under her head in such a way that her hair was not mussed by it — instead, it looked just as neat as if she were going to a party. And it was just as nice as a party, because they all had such a happy time together watching the new baby.

Bōt'Chan acted just like all the other babies in the world. First he got his fist into his mouth by accident, and sucked it. Then he got it out again without meaning to, and punched himself in the nose with it — such a funny little nose, no bigger than a small button! Then he opened his mouth wide and yawned.

"See how sleepy the little mouse is," said the Mother. "Run out and play now, my children, and let him rest."

Taro and Take left the room softly and went out on the porch. They sat down on the top step to talk over the wonderful thing that had happened.

It was springtime and the flowers in the

garden were just pushing their leaves
through the ground. The sun was shining,
and a little new yellow butterfly, that had
only just crept out of its snug cocoon that
very day, was dancing about in the sunshine.

"I suppose we were new once, too,
weren't we?" said Take, watching the
butterfly.

"I suppose we were," Taro answered.

"We grew right up out of the root of a tree. Natsu told me so."

"I wonder which tree it was," Take said.

"It must have been one of the trees in our own garden, of course," Taro answered; "or else we shouldn't be here."

"Wouldn't it have been a terrible accident if we had happened to grow in some other garden?" said Take. She looked quite scared just at the very thought of such a thing.

"Maybe if we had we shouldn't have been ourselves at all," Taro answered. He looked a little scared, too.

"Who should we have been, then?" asked Take.

"I don't know, I'm sure," Taro said. "I can't think. But, anyway, we're lucky that it didn't happen. We're here — and we're ourselves!"

"Let's go into the garden this minute and see if we can find Bōt'Chan's tree," said Take. "He's so new that maybe we can find the very spot where he grew."

"The fairies would surely hide the place so we could n't find it," said Taro; "but we can try. Let's go softly; then maybe they won't hear us."

They tiptoed out into the garden. How I wish you could see their garden! There are all sorts of wonderful places in it! It is n't very large, but it has in it a little bit of a toy mountain, and a tiny lake with little weeny goldfish in it, and a little stream of water, like a baby river, that runs into the lake. And, best of all, there is a curved bridge, painted red, just big enough for the Twins to walk over, if they are very careful and don't bounce! The Twins' Grandfather

made this garden for their Father to play
in when he was a little boy, so they all love
it dearly.

There are iris plants and lilies beside the
tiny lake, and a funny little pine tree—a
very little pine tree, just a few feet high—
grows out of some rocks on the side of
the mountain.

The Twins crossed the tiny red bridge
and crept up the stepping-stones on the
mountain-side until they reached the little
pine tree.

"Do you s'pose it could be the pine tree?"
Take whispered.

"Maybe; it's so small—just the right
size for Bōt'Chan," Taro whispered back.

The Twins looked carefully all around
the pine tree, but its trunk was gnarled and
old. It is hard to believe that so little a tree
could be so old, but the Japanese know how
to keep a tree small, like a toy tree, even if
it has been growing for a hundred years.

This tree wasn't a hundred years old,
because their Grandfather had set it out,

when the Twins' Father was a little boy,
and the Twins' Father was n't anywhere
near a hundred years old.

"I don't believe a darling little pink baby
could ever grow here," said Take, when she
had looked all around the pine tree. "Let's
look at the plum tree."

They ran to the plum tree that stood at
the other end of the garden. They looked
all about it.

On the south side of the plum tree, in the sunshine, there was a long branch near the ground; and on the branch — what do you think? — there was a whole row of tiny pink buds, almost ready to burst into bloom !

"Oh, Taro, Taro, look here !" Take cried. "Here 's the Baby's very own branch; I 'm sure of it, for there are n't any other buds on the whole tree that are as near out as these !"

"Let 's cut off this spray and carry it into the house to put in the vase," said Taro.

"Oh, yes, and I 'll show Mother how beautifully I can arrange it — just the way I was taught to do it," Take answered. "Nothing could be nicer for a baby's flower than a dear little branch like this with pink buds on it !"

"I 'll break it for you," said Taro. "I 'm strong."

He broke the branch carefully, just where Take told him to. He took great pains not to tear the bark or hurt the tree.

Then they carried it into the house. In

one corner of the room there was a little
alcove. There is one in every Japanese
house. It is called the "honorable recess,"

and it is where their most beautiful things
are placed. There is always a picture — or
perhaps two or three of them — hanging
like long banners on the wall at the back

of the "honorable recess." These banner pictures are called kakemono. There is also a small table with a vase on it standing near. In this vase there are always flowers, or a beautiful branch with green leaves. In Japan the little girls are taught to arrange flowers just as carefully as they are taught to read, so that the "honorable recess" may be kept beautiful to look at.

Take filled the vase with water. She fitted a little forked stick into the top of the vase, and stuck the plum branch through the crotch of the forked stick, so it would n't fall over. She twisted it this way and that until it looked just right. Then she called Taro to see it.

On the wall of the recess was the picture of a black crow perched on the branch of a pine tree, in a rainstorm. His shoulders were all hunched up to shed the rain, and he did n't look happy at all. He looked funny and miserable.

The Twins looked at the honorable recess a long time. Their Father came and

looked too. Then Taro said, "I don't think
that crow in the rainstorm looks right
hanging up beside the plum branch. The
crow looks so sorry, and we are all so
glad."

"I think just the same," said Take.

"So do I," said their Father. "How would you like to go out to the Kura and see if we can find a real happy picture to hang up there?"

Taro and Take jumped up and down and clapped their hands for joy, they were so glad to go out to the "Kura."

The "Kura" is a little fireproof house in the garden. You can see the corner of the roof sticking out from behind the mountain in the picture. In it Taro and Take and their Father and Mother and Grandmother keep all their greatest treasures. That is why Taro and Take were so glad to go there.

Nearly everybody in Japan has just such a safe little house in the garden. Maybe you can guess the reason why. It is n't only because of fires. It's because of earthquakes too.

Every once in a while—almost every day, in fact—the earth trembles and shakes in the Happy Islands. The houses are built mostly of wood and paper, and if the earthquakes tumble them over, they sometimes catch fire, but if the nicest things are safe in the Kura, it does n't matter so much, if the house is burned up, you see.

There are always plenty of fires for boys to see in Japan.

Taro had seen ever so many, before he was five years old, and the Twins had both felt ever so many earthquakes. They were so used to them that they did n't mind them any more than you mind a thunder-shower.

All of Taro's kites were kept in the Kura. The big dragon kite had a box all to itself; Take's thirty-five dolls were there, too; — but, dear me, — here I am telling you about kites and dolls, when I should be telling you about the picture of the crow, and what they did with it!

First the Twins' Father took it down off the wall and rolled it up. Then he took it in his hand, and he and Taro and Take all went out into the garden.

When they reached the Kura, the Father unlocked the door, and all three stepped inside.

It was not very light, but the air was sweet and spicy. On the shelves about the room were many beautiful boxes of all sizes and shapes.

The Father reached up to a high shelf and took down three boxes, that looked just alike on the outside. He opened the first and took out a roll neatly wrapped and tied with a silk string. It was this picture of a Japanese lady who has run out quickly to take her washing off the line because of a shower of rain.

He held it up high so the Twins could see it.

"Ho, ho," laughed Taro. "The lady has lost her clog, she is in such a hurry!"

"She's just as wet as the crow," Take said, "and I don't believe she feels a bit happier!"

"She'll be wetter still before she gets her washing in, won't she?" the Father

said. "The clouds seem to have burst just
over her head! And, dear me,—how the
wind is blowing her about! No, she won't
do beside the plum branch."

He opened another box and unrolled **the**
next picture. Here it is.

Taro and Take looked at it a long time.

Then Take said, " What a beautiful dress

the lady has on! I'd like to dress just like that when I grow up!"

"But she is walking out in the snow with an umbrella over her head," said Taro. " It is n't winter now."

Then the Father unrolled the third.

" How do you like this one?" he asked.

It was a picture of a bird with a grasshopper in her bill, flying to a nest with three little birds in it. The little birds had their mouths wide open.

"Oh, that's the very one!" cried Take. "It's just like Mother, taking care of Taro and the Baby and me! Let's take that one."

So they left that one out and carefully rolled up the others and put them back in place. They put the crow away too.

The Twins were just turning round to go out the door when their Father reached down one more package from a high shelf. "Wait a minute," he said; "I have something else to show you."

The package was long and thin, and the covering was a piece of silk with the family crest embroidered on it in colored silks.

This was the crest.

Taro and Take knew it at once, for it was embroidered or stamped upon the sleeves of their kimonos. It was the sign of their family.

The Father took off this cover. Under it was a covering of brocaded silk.

It seemed a long time to the Twins before it was all unwrapped, they were so eager to see what was in the package.

At last their Father held up a beautiful sword with both his hands.

It was a long sword, with a handle of carved ivory, and a sheath with curious designs on it.

The Father bowed to the sword.

"You bow to the sword also, my son," he said to Taro. " It is wonderfully made. It commands respect."

Taro bowed to the sword.

Then his Father drew the long blade from the sheath. He turned the edge carefully toward himself, and away from the Twins. "I want you to see this sword, Taro," he said, "for some time it will be yours, because you are my oldest son."

" Whose was it?" asked Taro.

" It was your Grandfather's sword," his Father answered, " and you are old enough now to know what it means. I want you to remember what I say to you as long as you live.

"Your Grandfather was a gentleman, a Samurai of Japan. This was the sword he always wore. Many years ago there was trouble in Japan, and to help the Emperor, all the great dukes in the kingdom gave up their dukedoms. The Samurai also gave up their honorable positions in the service of these dukes, and became common citizens.

Then your Grandfather put away his sword. Years after, when he was old, he gave it to me. But I do not wear it either, although I too am of the Samurai, and the sword is their badge of honor. It is much better to keep it safely here, and think sometimes of what it means, than to wear it only for display. You can show that you are a son of the Samurai, by acting as a gentleman should act. You do not need the sword for that. A Samurai should never do a mean thing. He should keep his life clean and shining, like the sword. And he must always do what is best for Japan, whether it is best for him or not."

This was a long speech. The Twins listened with all their ears, — four of them, — but they did not quite understand it all.

They understood that their Father loved the sword, and that some time it was to be Taro's, and that he must be a brave, good boy or he would not be worthy of it; and that was a good deal, after all.

"May I touch it?" Taro asked.

"You may take it in your own hands,"

35

said his Father. And he gave it to Taro
almost as tenderly as he had given Bōt'Chan
to Take that morning.

He showed him the polite way to hold
it, with the edge toward himself.

Then while Taro held the sword, his
Father said: "I want to tell you a poem
that our Emperor's father wrote while he
was Emperor, and by and by when you are
bigger I want you to learn it by heart. Then,
when you are a man, and look at the sword,
you will remember it. This is the poem: —

> "'There is no second way whereby to show
> The love of Fatherland,
> Whether one stand,
> A soldier under arms, against the foe,
> Or stay at home a peaceful citizen,
> The way of loyalty is still the same.'"

The Father's voice was very solemn as
he said this verse.

The Twins were quite still as he wrapped
the sword in its silken coverings and put it
back again on the high shelf.

This was a long time for Take to be quiet, but she was thinking. When their Father had locked the Kura and they were on their way to the house with the picture of the birds, she said to him, "Father, am I not a child of the Samurai, too?"

"Yes, my daughter," her Father answered, "but you are a girl. It is not your fault, little one," he added kindly. "We cannot all be boys, of course. But to the keeping of the Sons is given the honor of the Family. It is a great trust."

"Don't I do anything at all for the honor of my Family?" asked Take.

"When you are grown up you will marry and live with your husband's family and serve them in every way you can," her Father answered. "You will belong to them, you see. Now, you must just be a good girl and mind your Father and Grandmother, and Mother, and your brothers."

"I'm just as old as Taro," said little Take, "and I think I know just as much.

Why can't he mind me some of the time? I think it would be fair to take turns!"

"But Taro is a *boy*," said her Father. "That makes all the difference in the world. Japanese girls must always mind their brothers!"

"Must I mind Bōt'Chan, too?" asked Take.

"Yes, Bōt'Chan, too."

"Won't anybody ever mind me at all?" asked Take.

"When you get to be a mother-in-law, then you can have your turn," said her Father, smiling. "Your son's wife will obey you."

"Will my son obey me, too?" asked Take.

"No, you must obey him if he is the head of the house," her Father explained.

"It's a very long time to wait," sighed Take, "and nothing but a daughter-in-law to mind me at last."

Her under lip puckered a little and she frowned—a little frown—right in the middle of her forehead.

"Tut, tut," said her Father. "Girls and women should always be gentle and smiling. You must never frown."

He looked quite shocked at the very idea of such a thing.

Take tried to look pleasant, and a funny thing is that when you make yourself look

pleasant, you begin to feel so, too. Take felt
pleasant almost right away.

They went into the house and hung the
picture of the mother bird in the place of
the crow, beside the spray of plum. When
it was all done, this is the way the honorable recess looked.

"Take looked at it for a while, and then she said, "I don't believe I shall feel sorry about minding Bōt'Chan, after all, because I love him so much."

"That's the way a little Japanese girl should feel," said her Father. "Now, come in and let us take a look at him."

They found Bōt'Chan awake. Take knelt down on the mat in front of him, to see him better.

"Put your head down on the matting,

Take," her Father said, and Take bowed her head to the floor.

Then the Father took the Baby in his arms and placed his tiny foot on Take's neck.

"That means that you must always do what he wants you to," he said.

"I will," said little Take.

The Mother smiled at Take as she knelt on the floor with the Baby's foot on her neck.

Then she turned her face the other way on her little wooden pillow and sighed — just a very gentle little sigh, that nobody heard at all.

II

MORNING IN THE LITTLE HOUSE

II

MORNING IN THE LITTLE HOUSE

ONE morning when Bōt'Chan was just one month old, his big brother Taro woke up very early. The birds woke him. They were singing in the garden. "See, see, see," they sang. "Morning is here! Morning is here!" Taro heard them in his sleep. He turned over. Then he stretched his arms and legs and sat up in bed, rubbing his eyes.

The candle in the tall paper lamp beside his bed had burned almost out, but it was light enough so he could see that Take, in her bed across the room, was still asleep, with her head on her little cushion.

Taro called very softly, "Take, Take, wake up!" But Take slept so soundly she did not hear him.

Father and Mother and the Baby were
all asleep in the next room. He did not
want to wake them, because it was still so
early in the morning. So he crept softly
along the floor to Take's bed, and whispered in her ear, "Wake up, wake up!"
But she did n't wake up. Then Taro took

a jay's feather which he had found in the
garden the day before, and tickled Take's
nose!

First she rubbed her nose. Then she

sneezed. Then she opened her eyes and looked at Taro.

"Sh-sh," whispered Taro.

"But I have n't said a single word!" Take whispered back.

"You sneezed, though," said Taro. 'That's just as bad. It will wake up our honorable parents just the same."

"Well, you should n't tickle my poor little nose, then," said Take.

"Your honorable nose was tickled so that you would wake up and hear the birds sing," said Taro. "It is much nicer than sleeping! Besides, do you remember what is going to happen to-day? We are going to take Bōt'Chan to the Temple!"

A temple is something like a church, only they do not do the same things in temples that we do in our churches.

The Twins loved to go to the Temple, because they had a very good time when they went there. They liked it as much as you like Thanksgiving Day and the Fourth of July.

When Take remembered that they were going to take Bōt'Chan to the Temple, she clapped her little brown hands. "Oh, I'm so glad!" she said. Then she popped out from under the covers of her bed and stood up on the soft straw matting.

She was no sooner out of bed than from far away came the "*Cling — cling — clang*" of a great gong. And then, "*Tum — tum — t-r-r-rum*" rolled a great drum.

"Hark!" said Taro. "There go the Temple bells, and the priests are beating the sunrise drums! It's not so very early, after all."

"Now, you'll hear Grannie's stick rapping for the maids to get up," Take answered. "The Temple bells always wake her."

And at that very minute, "*Rat — tat — tat*" sounded Grannie's stick on the woodwork of the room where the maids slept.

In the little house in the garden where the Twins lived, there are no thick walls.

48

There are only pretty wooden screens covered with fine white paper. These screens
slide back and forth in grooves, and when
they are all shoved back at once the whole
house is turned into one big, bright room.
This is why the Twins had to be so careful not to make any noise. Even a tiny

noise can be heard all through a house that
has only paper walls, you see.

But every one is supposed to get up at
sunrise in the little house in the garden,
anyway.

The maids were stirring as soon as

Grannie called them. They rolled back the shutters around the porch and made so much noise in doing it that Father and Mother woke up too.

Then the Twins did n't keep so quiet any more. "I 'll beat you dressing," Take said to Taro.

She ran to the bathroom to wash her face and hands, and Taro ran to wash his in a little brass basin on the porch.

"Be sure you wash behind your ears, Taro," Take called to him. "And it 's no fair unless you brush your teeth hard!"

Taro did n't say anything. His tooth-brush was in his mouth, and there was n't room for words too. So he just scrubbed away as hard as he could. Then he ran back to his room and dressed so quickly that he was all done and out in the garden before Take began to put on her little ki-mono! You see, all Taro's clothes opened in front, and there was n't a single button to do up; so he could do it all himself — all but the sash which tied round his waist and held everything together. Take always tied this for him.

When Take came out into the garden she had her sash in her hand. Taro had his in his hand.

"I beat!" Taro called to her.

"You have n't got your sash on yet," Take called back.

"You have n't either," said Taro.

"We both of us did n't beat then," said Take. "Come here and I 'll tie yours for you."

Taro backed up to Take, and she tied his sash in a twinkling.

Then she held up her sash. "Now, you tie mine for me, Taro," she said.

"Wait until Mother can help you," said Taro. "Boys should n't do girls' work."

"Oh, please, Taro," said Take. "I tied yours for you. I don't see why you can't tie mine for me!"

"Well, you know what Father said," Taro answered. "He said you are a girl and must mind me. You get Mother to do it."

"He said you should be kind and noble, too," said Take. "It would be kind and noble of you to tie my sash, because I'm just suffering to have it tied." She looked at him sidewise. "Please do," she said.

Taro thought it over. Then he said, "Well, come behind the lantern, and just this once I'll do it. But don't you tell, and don't you ask me to again."

"Cross my heart, Taro," Take promised. "I won't tell. You are a good, kind boy."

Taro tied the sash the best he could, but it looked very queer. It looked so queer that when, after a while, their Mother saw it she said, "Come here, my child; your sash is tied upside down! But I know it is hard to reach behind you. I must teach you how to make a nice big bow all by yourself." And Take never told her that Taro did it. No one ever knew it until this minute!

When they were all dressed, the Twins ran out into the garden.

There had been a shower in the night,

and the leaves were all shiny, they had
been washed so clean by the rain. The
dew sparkled on the green iris leaves beside the tiny river, and the sunshine made
the fish look like lumps of living gold in
the blue waters of the little lake. The birds
were singing in the wistaria vine that grew
over the porch, and two doves were coo-
ing on the old stone lantern that stood by
the little lake. They were Taro's pet doves.

Taro held out his fingers. "I have n't
forgotten to bring you something," he called

The doves flew down and lit upon his shoulders. Taro took a few rice kernels from the sleeve of his kimono — which he used as a pocket — and fed the birds from his hand. They were so tame they even picked some from his lips.

"I will feed the fish too," Take said. And she ran to the kitchen where the maids were preparing breakfast. She came back with some white rice wafers in her fingers. First she threw some tiny bits of the wafer

into the water. The fish saw them and came to the surface. Then Take reached down and held the wafer in her fingers. The little fish came all about her hand and nibbled the wafer without fear. One of them even nibbled her finger!

Take laughed. "Mind your manners," she said to the little fish. "It's not polite to try to eat me up when I'm feeding you! I'm not your breakfast, anyway!"

Just then they heard the tinkling sound of a little gong.

"*Ting — ting — ting!*" sang Take to the sound of the gong. "Breakfast is ready." And she danced up the gravel walk to the house, her hair bobbing up and down, and her sash flying in the wind, so that she looked like a big blue butterfly.

Taro came too, and they sat down on mats in the kitchen, to eat their breakfast.

Their Mother was already serving their Father's breakfast to him in the next room. By and by she and Grandmother would have their breakfast with the servants.

This is a picture of the Twins eating their breakfast.

They each had a tiny table of red lacquered wood. On each table were two bowls. In one bowl was soup, and in the other rice.

Taro took up his soup-bowl with both hands. He was in a hurry.

"Oh, Taro!" Take said. "What would Mother say! You must be more polite. You *know* that is n't the way to hold your bowl."

Taro set his bowl down again, and took it up carefully with one hand, just as you see him in the picture.

Take began to eat her rice. She had two little sticks in her right hand. She used these sticks instead of a fork or spoon.

But Take was in a hurry too. She spilled a little rice on the front of her kimono!

Taro saw it. "You're just as impolite as I am," he said. "It's just as bad to spill as it is to hold your bowl wrong."

"Oh, dear me! Then we're both impolite," said Take. "What would Mother say!"

"She'd be ashamed of us," said Taro.

"Let's see if we can't remember every single one of our manners after this," said Take.

Just as they were finishing their rice there came the sound of steps — *Clumpity —clumpity—clump!*

"Who's coming?" said Taro.

"I think it's the hairdresser," Take answered.

She ran out to see. An old woman was on the porch. She had just slipped off her clogs.

58

In Japan no one thinks of such a thing as wearing street shoes in the house. It would bring in dirt and soil the pretty white mats. That was why she took them off.

Take bowed to the old woman. "Ohayo?" she said politely.

"Ohayo?" said the old woman to Take.

The Twins' Mother heard them. She came to the door. She bowed to the old woman, and the old woman bowed to her.

"Come in," said the Mother. "I hope you will make my hair look very nice to-day, because we are going to the Temple."

The old woman smiled. "I will make it shine like satin," she said.

The Mother got out her little mirror and sat down on the floor. The hairdresser stood behind her and began to take down the Mother's long black hair.

Bōt'Chan had been awake a long time. Taro was playing with him on the floor.

The Mother called Take. "Daughter," she said, "a little nap would make our baby wide awake and happy when we start for

the Temple. Would you like to put him to sleep?"

Take loved to put Bōt'Chan to sleep better than anything else in the world. She took him in her arms and hugged him close Then she swayed back and forth, and sang this little song: [1]

" How big and beautiful Sir Baby Boy is growing {

" When he becomes a good boy, too, then I will make our garden larger, and build a little treasure house for him.

[1] Adapted from translation by Sir Edwin Arnold.

"Next to the treasure-house I will plant pine trees. Next to the pine trees I will plant bamboo. Next to the bamboo I will plant plum trees.

" To the branches of the plum trees shall be hung little bells ! When those little bells ring, O Sir Baby Boy, how happy you will be ! "

She sang over and over, and softer and softer, about the little bells ; and by the time the hairdresser had finished the Mother's hair and gone away, Bōt'Chan was fast asleep.

Then Natsu put him down on some soft mats, and combed Take's hair.

Take stood still, like a brave little girl, though there were three snarls in it, and Natsu pulled dreadfully !

When every one was ready to go, they looked very splendid indeed. They all wore kimonos of the finest silk, with the family crest embroidered on the back and left sleeve. And Bōt'Chan had new clothes that Grannie and Mother had made especially for him to wear on his first visit to the Temple.

When everybody else was dressed and
ready, Natsu waked Bōt'Chan and put his
new clothes on him.

"Now, we can start," said the Mother.

She took Bōt'Chan in her arms. Natsu
slid open the door, and they all stepped out
on the porch.

III
HOW THEY WENT TO THE TEMPLE

III

HOW THEY WENT TO THE TEMPLE

THE Twins were just stepping into their clogs when the front gate opened, and what do you think they saw! In came trotting three grown men, each one pulling a little carriage behind him! They came right up to the porch. Take was just standing on one foot, ready to slip her other one into the strap of her clog, when they came in. She was so surprised she fell right over backward! She picked herself up again quickly, and hopped along, with one shoe on and one shoe off.

"Are we going to *ride?*" she gasped.

Her Father laughed. "Yes, little pop-eyes," he said; "we are going to ride to the Temple, and you and Taro shall ride in one rickshaw all by yourselves."

67

The name of these little carriages drawn by men instead of horses is "jinrickshas," but he called them "rickshaws" for short.

The Twins were so happy they could hardly keep still. They looked at all three rickshaws and all three men, and then they said to their Father: —

"May we ride in this one?"

It had red wheels.

"Yes, you may ride in that one," he said.

Then he got into the one with green wheels, and rode away.

Mother and Grannie and the Baby got into the next one, and their rickshaw man trotted away after Father.

"Keep close behind us," the Mother called back to the Twins.

They got into the rickshaw with the red wheels, and away they flew.

The Twins had never been in a rickshaw alone before in all their lives. They sat up very straight, and held on tight because it bounced a good deal, and the rickshaw man could run very fast.

"I feel as grand as a princess," Take whispered to Taro. "How do you feel?"

"I feel like a son of the Samurai," Taro whispered back. That was the proudest feeling he could think of.

There were so very many interesting things to see that the Twins did n't talk much for a while. You see, it 's hard work to use your mouth and your eyes and your ears all at once. So the Twins just used their eyes.

It was still quite early in the morn-

ing when they reached the city streets. Here they saw men with baskets hung from poles going from house to house. Some were selling vegetables, some had fish, and others were selling flowers, or brooms.

They saw little girls with baby brothers on their backs, skipping rope or bouncing balls The baby's head wobbled dreadfully

when his little sister skipped, but he did n't
cry about it. He just let it wobble!

The Twins rode by fruit-shops, and cloth-
ing-shops with gay kimonos flapping in
the breeze; by little shops where people
were making paper lanterns, by tea-shops
and silk-shops, by houses and gardens
in strange places they had never seen before.

They saw an old priest going from door to door, holding out his bowl for money.

In one street carpenters were putting up a new house, and once they caught a glimpse of the very bridge that leads to the Emperor's palace.

By and by they reached the gate of the

Temple grounds. All the rickshaws stopped here, and everybody got out.

The Mother put Bōt'Chan on her back, and they all started in a procession for the Temple. First walked the Father, looking very proud. Then came the Twins, looking quite proud, too. Then came Mother and Grannie and Bōt'Chan, and they looked proudest of all!

When they got inside the gate, the Twins thought they were in fairyland You would have thought so, too, if you could have been there with them.

They saw so many wonderful things that day that if I were to tell you about every one of them it would fill up this whole book!

First of all, they came into a broad roadway with beautiful great cedar trees on each side. Under these trees were little booths. Great paper lanterns and banners of all colors hung in front of the booths; and when they waved gayly in the wind, the place looked like a giant flower-garden in full bloom.

Near the Temple entrance was a great
stone trough full of clear water. There was
a long-handled wooden dipper floating on
it.

"Come here," said the Father.

The Twins, Grandmother, and Mother,
with Baby on her back, all came at once
and stood in a row beside the trough. They
put out their hands. The Father took the
dipper and poured water on their hands.

When their hands were quite clean, they rinsed their mouths, too. Then they entered the Temple vestibule.

There were more little booths in the Temple vestibule, and there were so many people, big and little, crowding about that the Father took the Twins' hands so they would n't get lost.

First he led them to a place where they bought some cooked peas on a little plate, and some rice. He gave the peas to Taro and some of the rice to Take.

The Twins wondered what in the world their Father wanted with peas and rice. They soon found out. In the very next place was a little stall, and in the little stall was a tiny, tiny white horse — no bigger than a big dog! Even its eyes were white.

"Oh, Father," the Twins said, both together, "*whose* little horse is it?"

"It 's Kwannon's little horse," the Father said. "Taro, you may give him the peas."

Taro held out the plate. The little white pony put his nose in the plate and ate them all up! He sniffed up Taro's sleeve as if he wanted more.

Take patted his back. "Who is Kwannon?" she asked.

"Kwannon is a beautiful goddess who loves little children," said the Father.

"Does she live here?" asked Taro.

"This is her Temple, where people come to worship," the Father answered. "We are going to pray to her to-day to take good care of Bōt'Chan always."

"Did you ask her to take care of us, too?" asked Take.

"Yes; we brought you both here when you were a month old, just as we are bringing Bōt'Chan now," the Father replied.

"Does she take care of *all* little children?" Take said.

"She loves them all, and takes care of all who ask for her protection."

"My!" said Take. "She must have her hands full with such a large family!"

Her Father laughed. "But, you see, she

has a great many hands," he said. "If she had only two, like us, it would be hard for her to take care of so many."

"I never saw her take care of me," said Taro.

"We do not see the gods," their Father answered. "But we must worship and obey them just the same."

"I think Kwannon must love little children," said Take, "because she wants them to have such good times in her Temple."

They said good-bye to the little horse, and walked through an opening into a courtyard beyond. The moment they stepped into the courtyard a flock of white pigeons flew down and settled all about them.

"Take may feed the pigeons," the Father said. "They are Kwannon's pigeons."

Take threw her rice on the ground. The pigeons picked it all up. So many people fed them that they were almost too fat to fly!

At another booth their Father bought

some little rings of perfumed incense. He
put them in his sleeve. His sleeves could
hold more things than all a boy's pockets
put together!

When they reached the great door of the
Temple itself, the Father said: "Now, we
must take off our shoes." So they all slipped
their toes out of their clogs, and went into
the Temple just as the bell in the courtyard
rang out with a great — *boom* — BOOM —
BOOM! that made the air shiver and shake
all about them.

The Temple was one big, shadowy room, with tall red columns all about.

"It's just like a great forest full of trees, is n't it?" Taro whispered to Take, as they went in.

"It almost scares me," Take whispered back; "it's so big."

Directly in front of the entrance there was another bell. A long red streamer hung from its clapper, and under it was a great box with bars over the top. On the box there perched a great white rooster!

The Father pulled the red streamer and rang the bell. Then he threw a piece of money into the box. It fell with a great noise.

"Cock-a-doodle-doo," crowed the rooster! He seemed very much pleased about the money, though it was meant for the priests and not for him. "The rooster is saying thank you," cried Take. "Hush," said her Mother.

Then the Father drew from his sleeve a little rosary of beads. He placed it over his hands, and bowed his head in prayer

while Grannie and Mother and Baby and the Twins stood near him and kept very still. When he had finished, a priest came up.

The Father bowed to the priest. "Will you show us the way to the shrine of Kwannon?" he asked.

Away off at the farther end of the Temple, the Twins could see a great altar. Banners and lanterns hung about it, and people were kneeling on the floor before it, praying. Before the altar was an open brazier with incense burning in it.

"Come this way," said the priest. He led them to the altar.

The Father took Bōt'Chan from his Mother, and held him in his arms. The priest said a prayer to Kwannon, and blessed the Baby. Then the Father threw incense rings on the little fire that burned in the brazier before the altar. Wreaths of smoke began to curl about their heads. The air was filled with the sweet odor of it. Some of it went up Bōt'Chan's nose. It smarted. Bōt'Chan did n't like it. He had behaved beautifully up to that time, and I am sure if the incense had n't gone up his nose he would have kept on behaving beautifully. But it did, and Bōt'Chan sneezed just as the priest finished the prayer.

Then he gave a great scream. Then another, and another. Three of them!

The priest smiled. But the Father did n't smile. He gave Bōt'Chan back to his Mother just as quickly as he could.

He said, "The honorable worshippers will be disturbed. We must go out at once."

They hurried back to the entrance and found their clogs, and the moment they were outdoors again, in the sweet, fresh air, Bŏt' Chan cuddled down on his Mother's back and went to sleep without another sound.

Near the Temple they found an orchard of cherry trees in full bloom. People were sitting under the cherry trees, looking at the blossoms. Some of them were writing little verses, which they hung on the branches of the trees. They did this because they loved the blossoms so much. Children were playing all about. Near by was a pretty little tea-house.

Grannie saw it first. "I am thirsty," she said.

"So am I," said Take.

"So am I," said Taro.

"We're *all* thirsty," the Father said.

Outside the tea-house, under the trees there were wooden benches. They sat down on these, and soon little maids from the

tea-house brought them trays with tea and sweet rice-cakes.

They sat on the benches and sipped their tea, and watched the people moving about, and looked up at the cherry blossoms against the blue sky, and were very happy, indeed.

The Mother had carried Bōt'Chan all the way on her back, so maybe she was a little tired. Anyway, she said to the Father : —

"If you and the Twins want to go farther, let Grannie and me stay here and rest. You can come back for us."

"Would you like to see the animals?" the Father asked the Twins.

Taro and Take jumped right up, and took their Father's hands, one on each side, and then they all walked away together under the blossoming trees to another part of the park.

In this part of the park there were cages, and in the cages were lions, and tigers, and monkeys, and zebras, and elephants, and all kinds of animals! There were birds, too, with red and blue plumage and beautiful golden tails. There were parrots and cockatoos and pheasants. Wild ducks were swimming in the ponds; and two swans sailed, like lovely white ships, to the place where the Twins stood, and opened their bills to be fed.

In the Father's sleeve was something for each one. Taro and Take took turns. Take fed the swans, and Taro fed the great

fish that swam up beside them and looked
at them with round eyes. When they saw
the food the fish leaped in the water and
fought each other to get it, and when they
ate it they made curious noises like pigs.

"I don't think they have very good manners," said Take.

By and by they came to a queer little

street. This little street must have been made on purpose for little boys and girls to have fun in, for there were all sorts of astonishing things there. There were jugglers doing strange tricks with tops and swords. There were acrobats, and candy-sellers and toy-sellers going about with baskets hung from long poles over their shoulders. It was almost like a circus.

The street was full of people, and every one was gay. The Twins and their Father had gone only a little way up the street when an old woman met them. She had a pole on her shoulder, and from it swung a little fire of coals in a brazier. She had a little pot of batter and a little jar of sweet sauce, a ladle, a griddle, and a cake-turner!

"Would you like to make some cakes?" she said to Take.

Take clasped her hands. "Oh, Father, may I?" she said.

The Father gave the old woman some money out of his sleeve. She set the brazier on the ground.

Then Take tucked her sleeves back, put
the griddle on the coals, poured out some
batter, and cooked a little cake on one side
until it was brown. Then she turned it over
with the cake-turner, and browned it on the
other side. Then she put it on a plate and
put the sauce on it.

My, my! but it was fun!

The first cake she made she gave to her
Father.

He ate it all up. Then he said, "Honorable daughter, the cake is the very best I ever had of the kind. I am sure your honorable brother would like one too."

The Japanese are so very polite that they often call each other "honorable" in that way. They even call things that they use "honorable," too!

So Take said very politely, "Honorable Brother, would you like one of my poor cakes?"

It would be impolite in Japan to call anything good that you had made yourself. It would seem like praising your own work. That was why Take called them "my poor cakes."

"I should like a cake very much," Taro said.

Take poured out the batter. She watched it carefully, to be sure it did not burn. When it was just brown enough she gave it to Taro.

Taro ate it all up. Then he said to Take, "Honorable Sister, I should like to eat six."

The Father laughed. "If you stay here

to eat six cakes, we shall not see the dolls'
garden," he said. "Take must have one
cake for herself, and then we will go on."

Take baked a cake for herself and ate it.
She called it a "poor" cake aloud, but inside she thought it was the very best cake
that any one ever made!

When she had finished, she and Taro and
the Father bowed politely to the old woman.

"Sayonara," they said. That means
"good-bye."

The old woman bowed. "Sayonara," she called to them.

The Twins and their Father walked on. They soon found the dolls' garden. In it were many tiny pine trees like theirs at home. There were little plum trees, and

bamboos, and a tiny tea-house in it. There was a pond with a little bridge, too.

"Oh!" cried Take, "if it only had little bells on the plum trees, this would be the very garden I sang about to Bōt'Chan; would n't it?"

She stooped down and peeped under the little trees.

"Let 's play we are giants!" she said to Taro.

"Giants roar," said Taro.

"*You* roar," said Take. "It would n't be polite for a lady giant to roar!"

"Giants are different. They don't have to be polite," Taro explained.

"Well, you can roar," said Take, "but I shall play I 'm a polite lady giant taking a walk in my garden! My head is in the clouds, and every step I take is a mile long!"

She picked up her kimono. She turned her little nose up to the sky, and took a very long step.

Taro came roaring after her.

But just that minute Take's clog turned on her foot, and the first thing she knew she was flat on her stomach on the bridge! She forgot that lady giants did n't roar.

Taro was roaring already.

Their Father was ahead of them. He jumped right up in the air when he heard the noise. He was n't used to such sounds from the Twins. He turned back.

"What is the matter?" he said.

He picked Take up and set her on her feet.

"We're giants," sobbed Take.

"Her head was in the clouds," said Taro.

"It is well even for giants to keep an eye on the earth when they are out walking," the Father said. "Are you hurt?"

"Yes, I'm hurt," Take said; "but I don't think I'm broken anywhere."

"Giants don't break easily at all," her Father answered. "I think you'll be all right if we go to your castle!"

"My *castle!*" cried Take. "Where is it?"

"Right over there through the trees." He pointed to it.

The Twins looked. They saw a high tower.

"Would you like to climb to the top with me?" their Father said.

"Oh, yes," Taro cried. "We are n't tired."

"Or broken," Take added.

So they went into the tower and climbed, and climbed, and climbed. It seemed as if the dark stairs would never end.

" I believe the tower reaches clear to the sky!" said Take.

" I don't believe it has any top at all!" said Taro.

But just that minute they came out on an open platform, and what a sight they saw! The whole city was spread out before them. They could see gray roofs, and green trees, and roadways with people on them. The people looked about as big as ants crawling along. They could see rivers, and blue ponds, and canals. It seemed to the Twins that they could see the whole world.

In a minute the Father said, " Look! Look over there against the sky!"

The Twins looked. Far away they saw a great lonely mountain-peak. It was very high, and very pale against the pale blue sky. The top of it was rosy, as if the sun shone on it. The shadows were blue. Below the top there were clouds and mists. The mountain seemed to rise out of them and float in the air.

The Twins clasped their hands.

"It is Fuji!" they cried, both together.

"Yes," said the Father. "It is Fuji, the most beautiful mountain in the world."

By and by Take said, "I don't feel a bit like a giant any more."

And Taro said, "Neither do I."

For a long time they stood looking at it. Then they turned and crept quietly down the dark stairs, holding tight to their Father's hands.

They went back to Mother and Grandmother and Bōt'Chan under the cherry trees.

"We must take the Baby home," said the Mother as soon as she saw them. "It's growing late."

"Oh, may n't we stay just a little longer?" Take begged.

"*Please*," said Taro.

"If we go now, we can go home by boat," said the Father.

"I did n't believe a single other nice thing could happen this day," sighed Take. "But going home by boat will be nicer than staying. Won't it, Taro?"

But Taro was already on his way to the landing.

There was a pleasure-boat tied to the wharf. The whole family got on board; the boatman pushed off and away they went over the blue waters and into **the** river, and down the river a long way, through the city and beyond. They passed rice-fields, where men and women in great round hats worked away, standing ankle deep in water. There were fields where

tea-plants were growing. There were little brown thatched roofs peeping out from under green trees. There were glimpses of little streets in tiny villages, and of people riding in a queer sort of basket hung from a pole and carried on the shoulders of two men.

At last they came to a landing-place

near their home. They were glad to see the
familiar roofs again.

Taro and Take raced ahead of the
others to their own little house in the
garden.

At the door they found ever so many
clogs. There were sounds of talking inside
the house.

"What do you suppose is going to happen now?" Take asked Taro.

"I don't know — but something nice,"
Taro answered, as he slipped off his clogs
and sprang up on the porch.

They slid open the door.

"Ohayo!" came a chorus of voices.

The room was full of their aunts and
cousins!

Taro and Take were very much surprised,
but they remembered their manners. They

dropped on their knees and bowed their
heads to the floor.

"Where are your Father and Mother,
and Grannie and Bōt'Chan?" said all the
aunts and cousins. "They are late."

"We came back by the boat, and it

stopped at ever so many places," said Taro. "That's why we are late."

Soon their Father and Mother and Grandmother came in. Then there was great laughing and talking, and many polite bows.

Bōt'Chan was passed from one to another. Everybody said he was the finest baby ever seen, and that he looked like his Father! And his Mother! And his Grandmother! Some even said he looked like the Twins!

Everybody brought presents to the baby. There were toys, and rice, and candied peas and beans, and little cakes, and silk for dresses for him, and more silk for more dresses, and best of all a beautiful puppy cat. Here is his picture! The Twins thought

Bōt'Chan could never use all the things that were given him but they thought they could help eat up the candied things.

Bōt'Chan seemed to like his party. He sucked his thumb and looked solemnly at the aunts and cousins. He even tried to put the puppy cat in his mouth. Natsu took him away at last and put him to bed. Then everybody had tea and good things to eat until it was time to go home.

It took the Twins a long time to get to sleep that night.

Just as she was cuddling down under her warm, soft mats, Take popped her head out once more and looked across the room to Taro's bed.

"Taro!" she whispered.

Taro stuck his head out, too. She could see him by the soft light of the candle in the tall paper lamp beside his bed.

"Don't you think it's about a week since morning?" she said. "So many nice things have happened to-day!"

"There never could be a nicer day than this," said Taro.

"What was the nicest of all?" Take asked. "I'll tell you what I liked the best if you'll tell me."

Then Taro told which part of the day he liked the best, and Take told which she liked the best. But I'm not going to tell whether they said the little horse, or the tiny garden, or the cherry trees, or the animals, or the boat-ride — or the party. You can just guess for yourself!

IV

A RAINY DAY

IV

A RAINY DAY

WHEN the Twins woke up the next morning it was cold, and the rain was beating on the roof. They could n't look out of the window to see it, because there were no glass windows in their house. There were just the pretty screens covered with white paper.

Taro slid one of the screens back and peeped out into the garden. "It 's all wet," he said to Take. "We can't play outdoors to-day."

"We 'll have a nice time in the house, then," said Take. "I can think of lots of things to do."

"So can I, if I try," Taro said.

"Let 's try, then," Take answered.

They thought all the time they were dressing. They put on three kimonos be-

cause it was cold. It made them look quite
fat.

"I've thought of one," Take called, just
as she was putting on the last kimono.

"I have, too," Taro said.

"You tell me and I'll tell you," Take
begged.

"No, not until after breakfast," Taro answered. "Then first we'll play one and
then the other."

After breakfast Mother was busy waiting upon Father and getting him off to his
work. Then she had to bathe the Baby.
So the Twins went to Grandmother for
help.

"O Ba San" (that means "Honorable
Grandmother"), Take said to her, "it is
rainy and cold, and Taro and I have
thought of nice games to play in the
house. Will you get the colored sands for
us?"

"I know what you're going to do!" cried
Taro.

Grandmother brought out four boxes.
In one box was yellow sand. In another
was black sand. The other two were filled
with blue and red sand. Grandmother
brought out some large pieces of paper.

"Thank you, O Ba San," the Twins
said.

They spread the paper on the floor. Taro
had one piece, and Take had another.

"I'm going to make a picture of a boat
on the sea," said Taro.

He took some of the blue sand in his
right hand. He let it run through his fingers
until it made a blue sea clear across the
paper.

"And now I'm going to make a yellow
sky for a sunset." He let the yellow sand
run through the fingers of his left hand.

"I'll put some red clouds in it," he said.

Then he let red sand run through his
fingers.

When that was done he took some black
sand. He made a boat.

This was the way his picture looked
when it was done, only it was in colors.
The sail of the boat was blue.

"Oh, Taro, how beautiful!" Take said.
"Mine won't be half so nice, I'm sure.
I'm going to make—I'm going to make
—let's see. Oh, *I* know. I'll make the
pine tree beside the pond!"

She took some blue sand and made the
little lake. Then she took the black sand
and made the trunk of the tree and some
branches.

She spilled a little of the black sand. It made black specks.

"Oh, dear!" she cried. "I 've spilled."

Taro looked at it. "Put the green leaves over the spilled place," he said.

"It is n't the right place for leaves," Take said.

She took some blue sand in one hand and some yellow in the other. She let them fall on the paper together. They made the green part of the tree.

"I know what I 'll do about the black that spilled," she said. "I 'll call it a swarm of bees! "

This is Take's picture. You can see the bees!

"I think your picture is just as good as mine," said Taro.

"Oh, no, Honorable Brother! Yours is much better," Take answered politely.

They showed them to Grannie when they were all finished. Grannie thought they were beautiful.

"Now, Taro, what's your game?" Take said when the sand was all put away.

"I have to go into the garden first for mine," Taro said.

"Put on your clogs and take an umbrella, and don't stay but a minute," Grannie said.

Taro put on his clogs and opened his umbrella, and ran into the garden.

Take couldn't guess what he wanted. She watched him from the door.

Taro ran from one tree or vine to another. He looked along the stems and under the leaves. He looked on the ground, too. Soon he jumped at something on the ground, and caught it in his hand.

"I've got one," he called.

"One what?" Take called back.

"Beetle," Taro said.

Then he found another. He brought them in very carefully, so as not to hurt them.

In the house he put them in a little cage which he made out of a pasteboard box. Then he got more paper and a little knife.

"Oh, Taro, what are you going to make?" Take asked.

"If you and grannie will help me, I'll

make some little wagons and we'll harness the beetles," Taro said.

"Won't it hurt them?" Take asked.

"Not a bit; we'll be so careful," Taro answered.

So Take ran for thread, and Taro got Grannie to help him. Grannie would do almost anything in the world for the Twins. And pretty soon there were two cunning little paper wagons with round paper wheels!

Taro tied some thread to the front of each little wagon. Then he opened the cage to take out the beetles.

One of the beetles did n't wait to be taken out. He flew out himself. He was big and black, and he flew straight at Take! He flew into her black hair!

Maybe he just wanted to hide. But he had big black nippers, and he took hold of Take's little fat neck with them.

Take rolled right over on the floor and screamed. Her Mother heard the scream. She came running in. The maids came running too to see what was the matter.

"*Ow! ow! ! ow ! ! !*" squealed Take. She could n't say a word. She just clawed at her neck and screamed.

Everybody tried to find out what was the matter.

"I know — I know !" shouted Taro.

He shook Take's hair. Out flew the beetle!

Taro caught him. "He is n't hurt a bit," he said.

"But I am," wailed Take.

Mother and Grannie bathed Take's neck, and comforted her; and soon she was happy again and ready to go on with the play.

She and Taro harnessed the beetles with threads to the little wagons. But Take let Taro do the harnessing.

"You can have that one, and I'll have this," Taro said; "and we'll have a race."

He set the beetles on the floor. They began to crawl along, pulling the little carriages after them.

Taro's beetle won the race.

They played with the beetles and wagons a long time until Grannie said, "Let them go now, children. Dinner will soon be ready."

The Twins were hungry. They unharnessed the beetles and carried them to the porch. They put them on the porch railing.

"Fly away home!" they said. Then they ran to the kitchen to see what there was for dinner. They sniffed good things cooking.

Take went to the stove and lifted the lid of a great kettle. It was such a queer stove!

Here is a picture of Take peeping into the kettle. It shows you just how queer that stove was.

"It's rice," Take said.

"Of course," said Taro. "We always have rice in that kettle. What's in this one?"

He peeped into the next kettle. It was steaming hot. The steam flew out when Taro opened the lid, and almost burned his nose!

That kettle had fish in it. When it was ready, Grannie and Mother and the Twins had their dinner all together. Bōt'Chan was asleep.

After dinner Grannie said, "I'm going for a little nap."

"We shall keep very quiet so as not to disturb you and Bōt'Chan," Taro said.

When the little tables were taken away, the Mother said, "Come, my children, let us sit down beside the hibachi and get warm."

The "hibachi" is the only stove, except the cook-stove, that they have in Japanese houses. It is an open square box, made of

metal, with a charcoal fire burning in it. In
very cold weather each person has one to
himself; but this day it was just cold enough
so the Twins loved to cuddle close up to
their Mother beside the big hibachi.

The Mother put on a square framework
of iron over the fire-box. Then she brought
a comforter — she called it a "futon" —
from the cupboard. She put it over the
frame, like a tent. She placed one large

cushion on the floor and on each side of the big cushion she put a little one.

She sat down on the big cushion. Taro sat on one side and Take sat on the other, on the little cushions. They drew the comforter over their laps — and, oh, but they were cozy and warm!

"Tell us a story, honored Mother," begged Taro.

"Yes, please do!" said Take.

"Let me see. What shall I tell you about?" said the Mother. She put her finger on her brow and pretended to be thinking very hard.

"Tell us about 'The Wonderful Tea-Kettle,'" said Take.

"Tell us about 'The Four and Twenty Paragons,'" said Taro.

"What is a Paragon?" asked Take.

"A Paragon is some one who is very good, indeed, — better than anybody else," said the Mother.

"Are you a Paragon?" Take asked her Mother.

"Oh, no," cried the Mother. "I am a most unworthy creature as compared with a Paragon."

"Then there are n't any such things," said Take, "because nobody could be better than you!"

The Mother laughed. "Wait until I tell you about the Paragons. Then you 'll see how very, very good they were," she said.

"Once there was a Paragon. He was

only a little boy, but he was so good to his parents! Oh, you can't think how good he was! He was only six years old. He was a beautiful child, with a tender, fine skin and bright eyes. He lived with his parents in a little town among the rice-fields. The fields were so wet in the spring that there were millions and millions of mosquitoes around their home. Everybody was nearly bitten to death by them. The little boy saw how miserable and unhappy his parents were from the mosquito-bites. He could not bear to see his dear parents suffer; so every night he lay naked on his mat so the mosquitoes would find his tender skin and bite him first, and spare his father and mother."

"Oh, my!" said Take. "How brave that was! I don't like mosquito-bites a bit!"

"You don't like beetle-bites any better, do you?" Taro said.

"Well," said Take, "I'd rather the beetle should bite me than Mother."

"Well, now, maybe you'll be a Paragon yourself sometime," the Mother said.

"There were n't any women paragons, were there?" asked Taro.

"Oh, yes," said the Mother. "Once there was a young girl who loved her father dearly, and honored him above everything in the world, as a child should. Once she and her father were in a jungle, and a tiger attacked them. The young girl threw herself upon the tiger and clung to his jaws so that her father could escape."

"Did the tiger eat her up?" said Taro.

"I suppose he did," the Mother answered.

"Was it very noble of her to be eaten up so her father could get away?" Take asked.

"Oh, very noble!" said the Mother.

"Well, then," said Take, "was it very noble of the father to run away and let her stay and be eaten up?"

"The lives of women are not worth so much as those of men," her Mother answered.

Take bounced on her cushion. "I don't see how she could honor a man who was so mean," she said.

Take's mother held up her hands. She was shocked. "Why, Take!" she said. "The man was her father!"

"Tell us another," said Taro.

"Please, honored Mother, don't tell me about any more Paragons," said Take.

Her Mother was still more shocked.

"Why, little daughter," she said, "don't you want to hear about the Paragon that lay down on the cold, cold ice to warm a hole in it with his body so he could catch some fish for his cruel stepmother to eat?"

"No, if you please, dear Mother," said Take, "because all the Paragons had such horrid parents."

"My dear little girl," the Mother said, "you must not say such dreadful things! We must honor and obey our parents, no matter what kind of persons they are."

"Well," said Take, "we love and honor you and our Father — you are so good and kind." She put her hands on the matting in front of her, and bowed to the floor before her Mother.

Taro saw Take do this, and he wanted to be just as polite as she was; so he rolled over on his cushion and bowed to the floor, too.

"Now, tell us about the 'Lucky Tea-Kettle,'" begged Take.

Their Mother began: "Once upon a time —"

But just as she got as far as that they heard a little sound from Bōt'Chan's cushion in the corner, and the covers began to wiggle.

"There's Bōt'Chan awake," said the Mother. "I must take care of him now. The 'Lucky Tea-Kettle' must wait until another time."

And just at that minute bright spots of sunshine appeared on the paper screen, and the shadows of leaves in pretty patterns fluttered over it.

"The sun is out! The sun is out!" cried the Twins.

They ran to the door, put on their clogs, and were soon dancing about in the bright sunshine.

125

V

TAKE'S BIRTHDAY

V

TAKE'S BIRTHDAY

TARO and Take loved their birthdays the best of all the days in the year.

They had two of them. Most twins have only one birthday between them, but Japanese twins have two.

That is because all the boys in Japan celebrate their birthdays together on one day, and all the girls celebrate theirs together on another day.

So, you see, though they were twins, Taro and Take did n't have the same birthday at all.

Take's birthday came first. She knew days beforehand that it was coming, for every once in a while she would say to her Mother, "How many days is it now?" and her Mother always knew she meant, "How many days is it to my birthday?"

One morning when she woke up, Take said, "Only six days more." The next morning she said, "Only five days more." One morning she jumped out of bed very early and said, "Oh, it's to-day! To-day! It begins this very minute."

Taro did n't get up early that day. When he heard Take singing, "It's to-day," he just buried his nose under the bedclothes and pretended to be asleep!

He remembered Take's last birthday, and he remembered that boys seemed to be in the way that day. They were n't asked to play with the girls, and they would n't have done it anyway, because the girls spent the whole day playing with dolls! Taro did n't think much of dolls.

Before breakfast, her Father took Take out to the Kura. He reached up to the high shelf and brought down the big red box that held the dolls. It was as big as a trunk. Then he reached down another box and carried them both into the house.

Although it was so early in the morning,

the Mother had already put fresh flowers in
the vase, in honor of Take's birthday.

The bedding had been put away, and on
one side of the room there were five shelves,
like steps against the wall. Take knew what
they were for.

"Oh," said Take, "everything is all ready
to begin! May I open the boxes right now?"

Her Mother said, "Yes." She even got
down on her knees beside the boxes and

helped Take open them. They opened the red box first. It was full of dolls! A whole trunkful of dolls. Thirty-five of them!

The first doll Take took out was a very grand lady doll, dressed in stiff silk robes, embroidered with chrysanthemums.

"Here's the Empress," she cried; she set the Empress doll up against the trunk. Then she ran to get her dear everyday doll. She called her everyday doll "Morning Glory," and sometimes just "Glory" for short. Glory was still asleep in Take's bed.

"Why, you sleepy head!" Take said. "Don't you know you are going to have company to-day? Where are your manners, child?"

She took Glory to the trunk and put her down on her knees before the Empress. "Make your bow," she said. Glory bowed so low that she fell over on her nose!

"Oh, my *dear* child!" said Take. "I *must* take more pains with you! Your manners are frightful! You will wear out your nose if you bow like that!"

She reached into the box and carefully
lifted out the Emperor doll. He was dressed
in stiff silk, too. He sat up very straight
against the trunk beside the Empress.

Take made Morning Glory bow to the
Emperor, too. This time Glory did n't fall
on her nose.

These dolls had belonged to Take's
Grandmother. She had played with them
on her birthdays, and then Take's Mother
had played with them on her birthdays, and
still they were not broken or torn; they had
been so well cared for.

They were taken out only once in the

whole year, and that time was called the
"Feast of Dolls."

Take's Mother had covered the five steps
with a beautiful piece of silk. Take placed
the Emperor and Empress in the middle of
the top step. Then she ran back to the
trunk to get more dolls.

There were girl dolls and boy dolls and
lady dolls in beautiful dresses, and baby
dolls in little kimonos, strapped to the backs
of bigger dolls.

Take took each one to the steps. She
made each one bow very low before the
Emperor and Empress before she put him
in his own place. All the shelves were filled
so full that one baby doll spilled over the
edge and fell on the floor! Take picked her
up and strapped her on Glory's back. "I
know *you* won't let her fall," she said to
Glory. Glory looked pleased and sat up
very straight and responsible.

Then Take opened the other box. She

took out a little stove and some blue-and-white doll dishes and two tiny lacquered tables.

While she was taking out these things, her Father brought in a new box that she had never seen before. He put it down on the floor before the steps. Take was so busy she did n't see it at first. When she did, she shouted, "Oh, Father, is it for *me?*"

"Yes, it is for you," the Father answered.

"Oh, thank you, whatever it is!" said Take.

She flew to the box and untied the string. She lifted the cover and there was a beautiful big toy house, made almost like the house the Twins lived in! It had a porch and sliding screens, and a cunning cupboard with doll bedding in it. It even had an alcove with a tiny kakemono, and a little vase in it! There was a flower in the vase! There were little straw mats on the floor!

Take lifted the mats and slid the screens

back and forth. She put her little stove in
the kitchen. She was too happy for words.
She ran to her Father and threw herself
on her knees before him and hugged his
feet. "Thank you, ten thousand times, dear
honored Father," she said.

When her own breakfast-time came, Take
was very busy getting breakfast for the
Emperor and Empress. She was so busy
she could n't stop. "It would n't be polite
for me to have my breakfast before the

Emperor and Empress have theirs," she explained.

Her Mother smiled. "Very well," she said, "You may get their breakfast first; we must be polite, whatever happens."

So Take had Morning Glory place the tiny lacquered tables before the Emperor and Empress. She put some rice in the little bowls on the tables. She placed some toy chop-sticks on the tables, too. Then she made Morning Glory bow and crawl away from the august presence on her hands and knees! "It would n't be at all right to stay to see them eat," she said.

Just then Taro came in, rubbing his eyes. He was still sleepy.

"Oh, Taro," cried Take, "look at my new house!"

"Taro did n't think much of dolls, but he liked that house just as much as Take did. When he saw the little stove with its play kettles, he said: "Why don't you have a *real* fire in it?"

"Do you think we could?" Take said.

Of course they were never, never allowed to play with fire, but because it was Take's birthday the Mother said, "Just this once I will sit here beside you and you may have three little charcoal embers from the tobacco-ban to put in the stove."

The tobacco-ban is a little metal box with a place for a pipe and tobacco. It always had a few pieces of burning charcoal in it so that the Father could light his pipe any time he wanted to. The Mother sat down beside the tobacco-ban.

She let Taro take a pair of tongs, like sugar-tongs. He put three pieces of charcoal in the tiny stove. Take put water in the kettle. Soon the water began to boil! Real steam came out of the spout.

"I can make real tea!" cried Take.

She got some tea leaves and put some in each tiny cup. Then she poured the boiling water into the cups. She put the cups of tea before the Emperor and Empress.

"Now you'd better have your own

breakfast," the Mother said. She put the fire out in the little stove and the Twins sat down before their tiny breakfast-tables.

While they were eating, Taro had a splendid idea. " I know what I 'll do. I 'll make you a little garden for your house ! " he said.

" Oh, that will be beautiful ! " cried Take.

The moment they had finished eating, they ran into the garden. Out by the well the maids were drawing water.

" I need some water, too," Taro said.

They let Taro draw a pail of water himself. Here is a picture of him doing it.

Then he found a box-cover — not very deep — and filled it with sand. He set a little bowl in the sand and filled it with the water, for a pond. Then he broke off little bits of branches and twigs and stuck them up in the sand for trees. He made a tiny mountain like the one in their garden and put a little bridge over the pond. He put bright pebbles around the pond. When it was all done, they put the garden down

beside the toy house. They put Glory in
the garden, beside the tiny pond.

But a horrible accident happened! Glory
fell over again, and this time she fell into
the pond! At least her head did. Her legs

were too long to go in. She might have been drowned if Take had n't picked her out in a hurry.

Just as Take was wiping Morning Glory's face, her Mother came in dressed for the street. She had Bōt'Chan on her back. He was awake and smiling.

Take ran and squeezed his fat legs. "You are the best doll of all," she said.

"You take your doll, and I 'll take mine," the Mother said, "and let us go for a walk."

Take had put on one of her very gayest kimonos that morning because it was her birthday, so she was all ready to go. Her Mother helped her strap Glory on her back and the two started down the street.

There were other mothers and other little girls with dolls on their backs in the street, too. They were all going to one place, — the Doll Shop! Each little girl had some money to buy a new doll.

Such chattering and laughing and talking you never heard! And such gay butterfly little dresses you never saw! nor such happy smiling faces, either.

At the Doll Shop there were rows and rows of dolls, and swarms and swarms of little girls looking at them. Take saw a roly-poly baby doll, with a funny tuft of black hair on his head. "This is the one I want, if you please," she said to the shopkeeper. She gave him her money. He gave her the doll.

"Glory," she said over her shoulder, "this is your new little brother!" Glory seemed pleased to have a little brother, and Take promised that she should wear him on her back whenever she wanted to. Take bought a little doll for Bōt'Chan, too, with her own money. It was a funny little doll without any legs. He was fat, and when any one knocked him over, he sat up again right away. She called him a "Daruma."

Bōt'Chan seemed to like the Daruma. He put its head in his mouth at once and licked it.

Just then Take saw O Kiku San. O Kiku

San was Take's best friend, and her home was not far from the little house where the Twins lived. O Kiku San had been to buy a doll, too. She had her new doll on her back. It was a large doll, with a red kimono.

She ran to speak to Take. "Won't you come into my house on your way home?" she asked.

"May I, Mother?" said Take.

Her Mother said, "Yes," so the little girls ran together to O Kiku San's house.

Other little girls came, too, to see O Kiku San's dolls. She had just as many dolls as Take. She had five shelves, too, and she had an Emperor and Empress doll. But she had no little house to play with.

"Come home with me and see my new house, all of you," Take said when the little girls had looked at O Kiku San's dolls.

So they marched in a gay procession to the little house in the garden. All the other girls' brothers had had a very lonesome day, but Taro had had fun all the afternoon with the little garden. He had made a little well, and a kura to put in the garden. He made them out of boxes. The little girls looked at Take's dolls. They thought the doll-house the most beautiful toy they had ever seen, and when they saw the garden, you can't think how happy they were!

"We wish our brothers would make gardens like that for us," they said.

Taro felt proud and pleased to have them like it so much, but all he said was, "It is very polite of you to praise my poor work!"

Then the Mother brought out some sweet rice-cakes. The maids brought out tiny tables and set them around. Take brought a doll teapot and placed it with toy cups on her little table. Then she made real tea, and they had a party! For candy they had sugared beans and peas. They gave some of everything to the dolls. It was nearly time for supper when the little girls bowed to Take and her Mother, said "Sayonara" very politely, and went home.

Take sat up just as late as she wanted to that night. It was eight o'clock when she went to bed. She hugged each one of the thirty-five dolls when she said good night to them.

"Sayonara, Sayonara," she said to each one; "good-bye for a whole year, you darling dolls!"

Then she took her dear old Glory and went happily to bed.

VI
GOING TO SCHOOL

VI

GOING TO SCHOOL

ONE morning Taro and Take heard their Father and Mother talking together. They thought the Twins were asleep, but they weren't. The Mother said, "Honored Husband, don't you think it is time Taro and Take went to school?"

"Yes, indeed," the Father said; "they have many things to learn, and they should begin at once. Have you spoken to the teacher yet?"

"I saw him yesterday," the Mother answered. "He said they might enter to-day. I have everything ready."

Taro and Take looked at each other.

"Do you suppose we shall like it?" Take whispered.

"I don't know," Taro whispered back. "I've liked everything so far, and I think going to school must be some fun, too. But of course, if I don't like it, I shall not say a word. A son of the Samurai should never complain, no matter how hard his lot."

"No, of course not," Take answered.

Before they were dressed, the Mother came into their room. "The bath-tub is ready, Taro," she said. "Hop in and get your bath early to-day, for you and Take are to begin school."

The Twins had a hot bath every day, but they usually took it before going to bed. The bath-tub was in a little room by itself. It was shaped a little like a barrel, and it had a stove set right in the side of it to heat the water. Taro went to the bath-room and climbed over the edge of the tub. It was hard to get up because the tub was high. He dropped into the water with a great splash. Take and her Mother heard the splash.

Then they heard something else. They heard screams! "Ow—ow—ow!" shrieked

Taro. "Take me out! take me out! I'm boiled!"

The Mother and Take ran as fast as they could to the tub. Taro's head just showed over the edge. His mouth was open, the tears were streaming down his cheeks, and the air was full of "ows." His Mother reached her arm down into the water.

"It is n't so very hot, Taro," she said; "I can bear my hand in it."

"Ow — ow!" said Taro. He did n't even say, "Ow! ow! Honorable Mother!" as one might have thought such a very polite boy would do.

And he tried to get both feet off the bottom of the tub at the same time!

The Mother put some cold water into the tub. Taro stopped screaming.

"Oh, Taro," Take called to him, "you are n't really and truly boiled, are you?"

"Almost," sniffed Taro; "I'm as red as a red dragon. I think my skin will come off."

"I know you are dreadfully hurt, poor Taro," Take said, "because a son of the Samurai never complains, no matter how hard his lot."

The water was cooler now. Taro's head disappeared below the edge of the tub. He splashed a minute, then he said: —

"I guess a real truly Samurai would scream a little if he were boiled." His words made a big round sound coming out of the tub.

Pretty soon it was Take's turn. She climbed into the tub. She splashed, too, but she did n't scream. Then she stuck her head over the edge of the tub.

"I 'm boiled, too," she called to Taro, "but I 'm not going to cry."

"Then the water is n't hot," was all Taro said.

When they had finished their baths, they were dressed in clean kimonos. Then they had their breakfast and at seven o'clock they were all ready for school.

Their Mother gave them each a paper umbrella in case of rain. She hung a little brocaded bag, with a jar of rice inside it, on the left arm of each Twin. This was for their luncheon. Then she gave them each a brand-new copy-book and a brand-new soroban. A soroban is a counting-machine.

It is a frame with wires stretched across it and beads hung on the wires. The Twins felt very proud to have sorobans and copy-books.

"Now trot along," the Mother said.

The Twins knew the way. They marched down the street, feeling more grown up than they ever had felt in all their lives. Their Mother watched them from the garden-gate.

When they turned the corner and were out of sight, she went back into the house. She picked up Bōt'Chan and hugged him. "Don't grow up yet, dear Sir Baby Boy," she said.

Taro and Take met other little boys and girls, all going to school, too. They all had

umbrellas and copy-books and sorobans.
The children got to the school-house before
the teacher.

They waited until they heard the *clumpty-
clump* of his wooden clogs. Then all the
children stood together in a row. Taro and
Take were at the end. The moment the
teacher came in, the children bowed very
low.

"Ohayo," they called. "Please make

your honorable entrance." They drew in their breath with a hissing sound. In Japan this is a polite thing to do. The teacher bowed to the children. Then each child ran to his little cushion on the floor and sat down on it. Taro and Take did not know where to go, because they had not been to school before.

The teacher gave them each a cushion. Then he placed beside each of them a cunning little set of drawers, like a doll's bureau. In the little bureau were India ink and brushes. The teacher sat down on his cushion before the school.

He told the children where to open their books. Taro and Take could n't even find the place, but O Kiku San, who sat next, found it for them.

The teacher gave Taro and Take each a little stick. "Now I will tell you the names of these letters," he said, "and when I call the name of each one, you can point to it with the little stick. That will help you to remember it."

He began to read. Taro and Take punched each letter as he called it. They tried so hard to remember that they punched a hole right through the paper! But you might have punched something, too, if you had thousands of letters to learn! That's what Taro and Take have to do, while you have only twenty-six letters. They were glad when the teacher said, "Now we will learn how to count."

Taro and Take took out their new sorobans. The teacher showed them how to count the beads. They thought it as much fun as a game.

Then they tried to make some letters in their copy-books with a brush. That's the way they write in Japan.

Taro's and Take's letters were very big and queer-looking, and the paper got so wet that the teacher said, "Children, you may all carry your copy-books outdoors and hang them up to dry, and you may eat your rice out of doors."

The children took their copy-books and

their bags of rice and ran out. The Twins
found a nice shady place to eat their
luncheon.

O Kiku San ate her rice with Taro and
Take. They had a real picnic.

At half-past three all their lessons were
finished, and the Twins ran home. Their
Mother was waiting for them on the porch,
with Bōt'Chan in her arms.

"See what we made for you!" the Twins
cried. They gave her the letters they had
made that morning.

"You have made them beautifully, for the first time," she said.

She put the blistered papers with the staggery letters away in the cupboard to keep. "I will show them to Father when he comes home," she said.

VII
TARO'S BIRTHDAY

VII

TARO'S BIRTHDAY

I wish there was room in this book to tell you about all the good times that Taro and Take have, but they have so many holidays and such good times on every one of them that it would take two books to tell about it all.

They have cherry festivals and wistaria festivals and chrysanthemum festivals when everybody goes to picnics and spends the whole day with the flowers.

On the day of the Lotus Festival they go very early in the morning, before the sun is up, to a pond where the lotus flowers bloom. They go with their teacher and all the children.

When they get to the pond, the teacher says, "Listen!" Every one is still as a mouse. Just as the sun comes up, the lotus flowers open. Pop, pop, pop, they go, like fairy guns! The children love to hear them pop. "The flowers salute the sun," they say.

One of the best days of all is New Year's Day, when all the boys and their fathers and grandfathers fly kites. And such wonderful kites! The air is full of dragons and boxes and all sorts of queer shapes. Sometimes the dragons have a battle in the air!

But one day I *must* tell you about, anyway, and that is Taro's birthday!

It is n't only Taro's birthday, you know. All the boys celebrate together. The girls —even if they are your very own twins— don't have a thing to do with it. And it lasts five days! On the first morning Taro woke very early. He was just as excited as Take was on the day of the Festival of Dolls. But Take did n't stay in bed on Taro's birthday. She flew out early, for she wanted to see all the fun, even if she was n't in it.

First she went to the Kura with Taro and their Father to get out the flags. The boys' birthday is called the Feast of Flags.

They took Bōt'Chan with them to the Kura. Take carried him on her back.

"It's Bōt'Chan's birthday, too," she said, "so he must go."

In the Kura was a long bamboo pole. The Twins' Father took the pole and set it up in the street before their house. Then he brought out two great paper fish. They were almost larger than Taro. They had great round mouths and round eyes. A string was fastened to their mouths.

"There's one fish for Taro and one for Bōt'Chan," said the Father. "We have two boys in our house."

He tied the fish to the pole. The wind filled the great round mouths and soon away up in the air the two fish were bobbing and blowing about just as if they were alive!

There was a bamboo pole with one or two — and sometimes three or four — fish on it before every house in the street!

" My! how many boys there are in the world!" Take said; "more than I can count!"

The street was as gay as a great flower-

garden. There were not only fish flags;
there was the flag of Japan, with a great
round red disk on it. And there was the
flag of the navy, which was a great round
red sun like the other, only with red rays
around it, and there were banners of all
colors waving in the breeze.

"Why are the fish flags all made just like the carp in the pond at the Temple?" asked Take.

"Because the carp is such a plucky fish," the Father answered. "He is n't a lazy fish that only wants to swim downstream, the easy way. He swims up the rivers and jumps up the falls. That's the way we want our Japanese boys to be. Their lives must be brave and strong, like the carp."

"And clean and bright like the sword, too?" Taro said.

"Yes," said his Father. "I'm glad you remember about the sword."

When the fish flags were bobbing about in the air, the Father and children went back into the house.

There were the steps in the side of the room again, just where they were when Take had her birthday. And Taro had his dolls, too. They were not like Take's. They were soldier dolls, enough for a whole army. Taro set them up in rows, as if they were marching! There were General dolls, and officers on horseback, and bands. There were even two nurses, following after the procession. There were toy guns, and ever and ever so many flags all in a row.

Taro was so excited he could hardly eat any breakfast! As soon as he had finished, he sprang up from his cushion. He almost upset his table, he was in such a hurry. He put on a play uniform like a soldier. And he had a wooden sword!

"There's going to be a war!" he said to Take.

"Where?" asked Take; "can I see it?"

"It's going to be in the street. I'm the General," said Taro.

"Oh, how I wish I could be a General," cried Take.

But Taro never even heard her. He was already on his way to join his regiment.

In a few minutes Take heard the "*rap-a-tap, tap! rap-a-tap, tap!*" of a drum. "They're coming! They're coming!" she called to her Mother and Father. The Mother rolled Bōt'Chan on to her back.

Take took her Father's hand. They all ran
to the gate to see the procession. The servants came out, too, and last of all Grannie.
They gave Grannie the best place to see.
Soon around the corner came the procession.

First marched a color-bearer with the
big Japanese flag. Then came Taro. He
looked very proud and straight, walking
all alone at the head of the procession. He
was the General because he had a sword!

All the boys carried flags. They kept
step like little soldiers.

"Oh, does n't Taro look beautiful?" said
Take. She climbed up on the gate-post.
She waved a little flag with all her might,
but Taro never looked round. He just
marched straight along.

Just then "*rub-a-dub-dub*" came the
sound of another drum. Around the next
corner came another army of little boys.

They carried flags, too. They marched
straight toward Taro's army.

"Now the war is coming! Now the war is coming!" shouted Take.

All at once Taro's soldiers began to run. The other soldiers ran, too. They ran straight toward each other and tried to get each others' flags.

Take saw Taro wave his sword. "On, soldiers, on!" he shouted.

Then there was a great mix-up of boys and flags. It seemed like a bundle of waving arms and legs and banners. Every boy was shouting at the top of his voice.

Take climbed right on top of the gate-post, she was so excited. She stood up on it and waved her arms!

"Look at that child," cried the Mother. "She'll fall."

Take was dancing for joy.

"There they come! There they come!" she cried.

Her Father reached up and held her still. "Be *quiet*, grasshopper," he said.

"But Taro is coming! They beat, they beat!" cried Take.

Taro and his army were coming up the street on the run. Nearly every little boy had two flags! The other army was running away as fast as it could go. They had only two banners left.

"Beat the drum!" shouted Taro. The drummer boy began, "*rat-a-tat-tat*," and the whole victorious army marched down the street and right into Taro's garden!

As he passed his Father and Mother and Grannie and Bōt'Chan, Taro saluted. His Father saluted Taro, and every one of the family — Grannie and all — cried "Banzai! Banzai!" That means the same as hurrah!

Then Take tumbled off the gate-post and raced up to the porch after the soldier. At the porch, the soldiers broke ranks.

The General's Mother ran into the house and brought out sweet rice-cakes and sugared beans. She fed the entire army. There were six boys in it.

"Fighting makes a soldier very hungry," Taro said.

Then his Mother went into the house and

brought out more cakes and more beans. The boys ate them all.

The army stayed at Taro's house and played with his soldiers and drilled on his porch until lunch-time, when they all went to their own homes.

After luncheon Taro played with his tops. He had two beautiful ones. One was a singing top.

He was spinning the singing top when all of a sudden there was a great noise in the street. He ran to see what was the matter.

There, almost right in front of his own house, was a real show! There was a man and a little boy and a monkey! The monkey had on a kimono. The monkey and the little boy did tricks together. Then the man and the boy did tricks. The man balanced a ladder on his shoulder. The little boy climbed right up the ladder and hung from the top of it by his toes.

Every boy in the street came running to see them. Take came, too. The little boy, hanging from the top of the ladder, opened a fan and fanned himself! Then he climbed to his feet again and stood on one foot on the top of the ladder. Then he made a bow!

Taro and Take almost stopped breathing, they were so afraid the little boy would fall.

The little boy threw his fan to the monkey. The monkey caught it and fanned himself, while the little boy came down the ladder to the ground, all safe and sound.

The Twins' Mother came out, too. She saw the little boy. She felt sorry for him. She felt sorry for the monkey, too. "Come in and have some rice-cakes," she said.

The man, the boy, and the monkey all came into the garden of the little house. All the other children came, too.

The Mother brought out cakes and tea. Everybody had some. The man and the boy thanked her. They made the monkey thank her, too. He got down on his knees and bowed clear to the ground.

When they had eaten the cakes and drank the tea, the man and the boy said, "Say-

onara, Sayonara." The monkey jumped on the man's shoulder, and away they went down the street, with all the boys following after.

Taro and Take did not go with them, because their Mother said, "It is almost time for supper." They watched the others from their gate. Then they came back and sat down on the top step of the porch.

"I think you 've had just as good a time on your birthday as I had on mine," Take said.

"Better," said Taro.

"Taro, we are getting very old, are n't we?" Take went on.

"Yes," said Taro, "we are six now."

"What are you going to be when you are seven or eight years old and grown up?" asked Take.

"Well," said Taro, "I 'm not sure, but I think I shall be either a general or a juggler," Taro said. "What are you going to be?"

"There 's only one thing I can grow

to be," said Take. "If I am very, very good, maybe I 'll grow to be a mother-in-law sometime."

Just then they heard their Mother's voice calling them to supper. It was very late for supper — it was really almost night.

The shadows in the little garden were growing long. The birds were chirping sleepily to each other in the wistaria vine. The iris flowers were nodding their purple heads to the little goldfish in the pond. Everything was quiet and still.

The Twins stopped to look at the little garden before they went in to their supper.

"Good night, pretty world," they said, and waved their hands.

THE END